THE WITCH ON THE CORNER

The Witch on the Corner

by Felice Holman

illustrated by Arnold Lobel

W · W · NORTON & COMPANY · INC · *New York*

For Anne,
who has a
green thumb, too.

CONTENTS

Just Something About Witches in General

Some people are celebrities — very
important — and are known far and wide for
their good works, their cleverness, or whatever.
They are often busy going places in
airplanes — here today, there tomorrow — (and that's
all very well and good). But, on the
other hand, there are some people who are much
more private and are known only around
their own neighborhoods.

And, of course, it is the same way
with witches. Some witches have more publicity
than others. They are always going hither
and thither on brooms and doing showy
bits of magic and so forth (and that is nothing
against them). But this story is about
a more private witch — a neighborhood witch,
in fact — named Miss Pinchon.

From the Outside of the Hedge Looking In | I

The witch on the corner lived in a tilting farm-house that looked as if it certainly could not stand another day. But around it, and surrounded by a thick hedge, was a big and beautiful garden in which the witch grew giant dahlias, double chrys-anthemums, hybrid roses, and countless other spectacular species, even when everyone else's gardens were wilted with drought, burned by the sun, or withered with frost.

The witch, Miss Pinchon, spent most of her time from dawn until the dew fell working in her flower beds. She worked, bent like a hairpin, grey head between black boots, planting, weeding, and poking about for hours and hours at a time. Any spare time she had, she devoted to keeping all living people out of the garden. It mattered not if it was a small boy sneaking grapes or an innocent stranger stopping to admire the flowers, Miss Pinchon stood with raised rake and muttered to go away.

A neighbor, Mrs. Hutchmaier by name, said she had actually seen the witch planting poison ivy on the stone wall between their houses. Mrs. Hutchmaier let it be known. And of course she told her own son, Zigmund, so that he would not climb on the stone wall anymore when he was plundering Miss Pinchon's garden.

Oh, there was plenty *said*. The child Marilla Dark, making the rounds with her father, the letter carrier, had actually seen the witch's fingers snatching the letters as they came through the slot. Her fingers were *green*. There were some who said she absolutely disappeared in the winter. She was there, they said, but invisible!

But Mrs. Geordi, who was new in the neighborhood, was very indignant when her children, Jacques and Lucy, told her about the witch on the corner.

"Nonsense!" she said. "Just as soon as I can, I shall go and call on her. She is probably just too old to come and call on me."

And she did. She dressed up in her afternoon calling clothes, put on white gloves, and walked up the road to the corner. She went up the path to the witch's house and rang the bell. There was no answer. She rang again. Then she rang again. Whereupon the door opened very fast, and before Mrs. Geordi could say how do, the witch had thrown a bucket of water out on that kindly caller.

Most of the children taunted Miss Pinchon. "Witch! Witch!" they would cry (but not too loudly). When she was bent over like a croquet wicket in her garden, Zigmund Hutchmaier had more than once pitched a rubber ball perfectly through the arch. Getting the ball back later in the dark was one of the things Zigmund was good at, and he usually managed a big chrysanthemum or two while he was about it.

Another sport was to wait until Miss Pinchon had backed up close to the front hedge while weeding, and then to blow a very loud horn. The pleasure of shocking Miss Pinchon was great, indeed, though it took a sturdy soul to stand by for more than a second after the horn blew. Miss Pinchon would swivel around and glare through the hedge, muttering and stamping, and even brave Zigmund would run screaming down the road.

But there was another small group of children — Lucy Geordi was one of them — who did not think it was at all nice to devil Miss Pinchon. These children would sit quietly in front of the

hedge with a big sign which read:

PLEASE DO NOT TAUNT THE WITCH

"Humanitarian!" teased Zigmund one day as Lucy sat with her sign. "Humanitarian!"

"I am not!" protested Lucy.

"You are! You are! You're a soppy humanitarian."

"I am *not* a hum-human-i-tarian," sobbed Lucy, and she ran home crying.

Zigmund picked up the sign she had dropped and crossed out PLEASE DO NOT. The sign now read TAUNT THE WITCH, and Zigmund added 1¢.

"How come it's one cent?" asked Jacques Geordi as he came by for his daily taunting. "I always did it for nothing."

"It's organized now," said Zigmund. "One cent. It's your dues. Taunting costs now."

One morning in the bitter winter, when it was

known that the witch was invisible, Zigmund saw a terrible sight. There she was on the back porch . . . bent double over the porch rail . . . and seemingly *headless*!

"The witch is dead!" screamed Zigmund, rousing late sleepers and summoning others from their breakfasts. "The witch is dead! Come see!" and he led the neighbors, clad in bathrobes, boots, and curlers, across the snowy paths and right up to Miss Pinchon's hedge. There they crouched beneath and craned above the hedge

to see what was to be seen. Mrs. Hutchmaier couldn't see very well because she was too vain to wear glasses and needed them badly. Mr. Hutchmaier couldn't see well because he was wearing his reading glasses (since Zigmund had called just as he was reading the morning paper) and the children were all too short to get a really good view. So it was Mr. Geordi, coming up last, who said he'd go see, though Mr. Dark warned him it was trespassing, and Mrs. Dark said maybe it wasn't any of their business.

Mr. Geordi pushed his way through the hedge and tiptoed into the backyard. The air was still and bitter cold, and Mr. Geordi was chilly in his bathrobe. There was no sound from anyone as he crossed the now bleak garden and went up the backyard path. He had almost arrived at the back porch when, from inside the house, a raucous screaming began. "Thief! Thief!" And then came a furious pounding on the inside of the back door, which put the fear into Mr. Geordi, just as he glimpsed the sight on the back porch. He turned and sped through the hedge.

"It's her nightgown! She must have hung it

on the rail to dry," he sputtered. "It's frozen stiff by the weather!"

At that news, Mr. Hutchmaier turned and whacked Zigmund a solid thump and growled, "Dead is she! Get off to school. At once!"

Zigmund was petulant all day. "Is that fair?" he asked all his friends. "If she had been dead, I wouldn't have gotten whacked would I? But she's *alive*, so they whack me!"

The Mr. Boo
Incident

II

Now, we have said that the Hutchmaiers lived on one side of Miss Pinchon. On the other side was a little woods — more of a bramble patch, really, with a few old trees. And on the far side of the little woods was Mr. Boo. Mr. Boo (really Mr. Bodenheimer) had lived on his land all his long life, and for twenty years of that time a certain cow had lived there too, and still did. All Mr. Boo's days were the same. They started at sunup when he went into the little barn and led the very old cow by a rope, out of the barn, and down the hill into the little pasture. And day in and day out, as they went down the hill, the cow, from habit, always gave Mr. Boo a good kick at the first opportunity. Whereupon Mr. Boo, also from habit, wheeled on the cow and kicked her back. Then they went on down the pasture together. It was an enduring relationship.

Then Mr. Boo went into his vegetable garden and hoed the rows of potatoes, corn, and squash. The rest of the day he walked the borders of his land, checking the fences and walls, and chasing stray dogs. He was particularly determined to keep the dogs away, because they bent the grasses of his pasture and made them hard to cut when it was time to bring in the hay for the cow. He was relentless in his pursuit of them.

The closeness of Mr. Boo's property to Miss Pinchon's was a real convenience to the neighborhood children, because just walking home from school, for instance, it was possible to taunt the witch a bit and then hide behind a tree and bark at Mr. Boo. The thought that there was still another dog on the place would animate

Mr. Boo in such a way that it gave a great deal of delight to the children. It was worth almost any risk involved.

The day that Mr. Boo and Miss Pinchon met started out like any other day — Mr. Boo led Estella to pasture with the usual exchange of kicks. Miss Pinchon, as usual, was bent over in the garden, thinning perennials. It was an early fall day and the morning was bright and nippy. Mr. Boo's squashes were big as the sun while Miss Pinchon's chrysanthemums lorded it over the neighborhood.

What happened was that it must have been a bit chilly in the pasture for the cow, and that made her feel like wandering. Wander she did, pushing over a stile that Mr. Boo had left a little less secure than usual, and ambling on into the little wood, where for a while she found something or other to her taste. She mosied around in there for a bit, nibbling at this, nibbling at that, aimless, but more or less content, and finally emerged on the other side of the wood at the sunny edge of Miss Pinchon's garden, where the Lady Perchpetal chrysanthemums were bursting themselves with pride.

Estella tasted one and loved it. It had a strange and exotic flavor quite unlike hay or grass. The cow was old, but not too old to cultivate a new taste, and so she was enjoying her second row of chrysanthemum heads when Miss Pinchon unbent herself from her usual horseshoe shape and turned around.

No one heard what she said, but Mrs. Hutchmaier just happened to come to her upstairs window and see Miss Pinchon reach for the broom on the nearby porch and start at a very good clip across the garden. (Now, Zigmund said she *flew* on the broom, but that is really just a rumor not to be confused with fact.)

At about that time, Mr. Boo, who had discovered that Estella was missing, finished searching the small woods and was poking his head tentatively into the hedge about Miss Pinchon's garden. The cow had become aware of some bustle around her, but old cows are slow to panic, and the sight of Miss Pinchon pelting across the garden swinging a broom did not unduly alarm her. This gave Miss Pinchon plenty of time to aim.

When Mr. Boo saw Estella, he gave a low calling whistle, at which Estella turned and started to amble toward Mr. Boo, and Mr. Boo started to move toward Estella. At just that moment Miss Pinchon closed in, and giving the broom a nice free swing, brought it down where she judged Estella to be. Unfortunately that spot was occupied by Mr. Boo.

Mrs. Hutchmaier reported that at first nobody moved except the cow, who had found another tasty group of flowers and was unaffected by the tragedy. Miss Pinchon remained still as a statue, apparently a bit taken aback, and from all appearances Mr. Boo was entirely unable to move.

Then, in very slow motion, Miss Pinchon bent

over Mr. Boo and began fanning him with the
broom. Then she picked up a nearby watering
can and sprinkled him a bit. Mr. Boo sat up.

Here, regrettably, this report gets a bit ragged.
Mrs. Hutchmaier *said* Mr. Boo muttered something and then Miss Pinchon muttered something, but anyone can see the weakness in this,
for, without malice toward Mrs. Hutchmaier,
there is surely some doubt about her ability to
hear muttering from a distance of three-hundred

yards, and it must also be remembered that she would not wear glasses.

On the other hand, given the combination of Mr. Boo, a known cow-kicker and dog-chaser, and Miss Pinchon, an established neighborhood witch, one would be led to expect some sort of temperamental display.

But whatever occurred between them, after a few moments Mr. Boo got to his feet and led Estella off through the hedge, through the field, and back to the barn. And Miss Pinchon stamped back to her house, dragging the broom behind her.

Zigmund was outraged when told of the episode. "What kind of witch is that!" he complained. "Couldn't she have turned him into a dog, at least?"

From the Inside of the Hedge
Looking Out | III

For as long as she could remember, nothing that Miss Pinchon did had ever gone right — except for her flowers. With flowers she could do no wrong and she knew it. She took enormous satisfaction in that fact, and the vague discomfort, way down inside, that otherwise she could scarcely do anything right, grew less and less as the years went along. Making flowers grow became her only real interest and she came to believe that people were other people's business. Not that she was bitter, but facts are facts, and it had been adequately shown over the years that Miss Pinchon did not have a green thumb where people were concerned.

It wasn't only people, either. It was things. Things became animate when Miss Pinchon touched them and acted quite independently of her good intentions toward them. So it was that Miss Pinchon found herself throwing a pail of water on a caller when she was dumping a wash-bucket. The fact was that because the doorbell didn't work she had no idea that anyone at all was on the porch. Well, there you are! And she hit a neighbor on the head with a broom when she was aiming at something else entirely . . . and quite justifiably, it might be added.

Miss Pinchon was quite used to salting her tea by mistake. She had grown to like it, as a matter of fact, quite as well as sugared. She took it as a matter of course that the stove exploded when she lit it, that the food burned, that the hot water came out of the cold-water tap. Since everything that ran on electricity either gave her a dreadful shock or broke down completely, she thought it

best, all things considered, to do without electricity and light her house with candles. A draft
down the stairwell made the candles flicker and
waver, and at night the house was shadowy and
eerie. The shades at the windows had ripped
long ago, and Miss Pinchon solved that problem
by letting the windows get quite dirty outside,
and on the inside she grew ivy geranium in a
great jungle over each window. From the outside of the house at night, the flickering candles
silhouetted the thick fluttering growth of ivy
geranium and created an effect that disturbed
the neighbors a great deal.

"It's very bad for property values," Mr. Hutchmaier complained.

"Living next to a witch is worse than living next to a graveyard," grumbled Mrs. Hutchmaier.

Miss Pinchon kept, or perhaps was kept by, an enormous parrot of strong and determined spirit. "Do be quiet," the parrot would say irritably, if Miss Pinchon muttered to herself a bit while doing up the breakfast dishes. She liked to talk while washing the dishes because it took her mind off the fact that sooner or later during the washing up she would, of course, break at least one dish.

In the evening, and during most of the winter, Miss Pinchon varied her activities between rocking very athletically in her old straw rocker or reading aloud from one of her two books, *Grimm's Fairy Tales* and *Pride and Prejudice*, which she had read over and over again for years.

Gideon, the parrot, would say "Oh, go to bed!" and force Miss Pinchon to retire early even when she would rather stay up and finish a particularly exciting story. But there was no point in arguing with Gideon because he would set up such a squawk that reading was out of the question anyway. On stormy mornings, when one couldn't get out into the garden and Miss Pinchon would have liked to stay in bed late, the parrot would scream "Get up, get up, get up!" and Miss Pinchon would not be able to sleep another wink.

But, despite it all, she was attached to Gideon, and though she found him irritating at times, he was a great companion to her; and in her heart she knew that she, too, was a bit irritating.

33|

It is hard to say just exactly when Miss Pinchon first began to realize she was a witch. But realizing made all the difference. Something somebody said to somebody else when Miss Pinchon was making one of her infrequent shopping trips to the grocery store . . . nibbling the crackers, snapping the beans, tasting the cheese, pinching the bread. Catching a word here and a word there, hearing the children at their taunting. And then one day Gideon shouted at her in a rage, "Witch! Witch! Witch!"

Miss Pinchon began to add it all up, and slowly, very slowly, it dawned on her . . . the astounding, the terrible, and finally the marvelous truth. "I'm a witch!" she whispered aloud. "I'm a witch! But, of course! That explains *everything!*"

Miss Pinchon rocked up a storm that night, and though Gideon shouted and complained, she rocked on, going over her life and explaining it all now that she saw herself as a witch. "Of course," she muttered half to herself and half to Gideon, "nobody loves a witch. That's why people have never been attracted to me. Witches usually associate with other witches. And notice how the glasses fly out of my hands and crash to the kitchen floor? Notice how the electricity used to spark and flash when I used it? It's a spell, that's what! Well, well! That puts a different complexion on things, doesn't it, Gideon?"

"Go to bed," said Gideon.

Miss Pinchon Tries Her Hand | IV
at Witchcraft

The next morning when Miss Pinchon went out into the garden to weed, rake, and hoe, she could have been heard humming, but no one was awake to hear her. She heard herself, however, and felt surprised and cheerful. "I have a very decent voice," she mumbled to herself. "Deep, but very decent. I shall have to do a few voice exercises from time to time."

Miss Pinchon was impatient all day. For the first time in her recollection gardening did not thrill and stir her and fill her completely. She had something on her mind. She cooked herself a good supper — or at least it had sounded good in the old cook book, but it turned out just like most of Miss Pinchon's cooking efforts — a gar-bled-looking stew. But it was wholesome and she wanted strength for her evening's activities. She cracked a cup while she was washing the dishes and exclaimed triumphantly, "Aha!"

When the birds had roosted for the night and darkness was well settled in, Miss Pinchon went out to the back porch and looked stealthily about. Not a soul in sight. Not a sound. The lights in the upstairs rooms of the neighboring houses suggested that people were preparing for bed. Miss Pinchon reached for the broom behind the back door and went out into the garden. She stood in the shadow of the big apple tree and, still looking about nervously, straddled the broom.

Miss Pinchon waited expectantly. She waited a long time, shifting her weight from one foot to the other. She took some deep breaths, more to quiet her pounding heart than anything else, and

waited a while more. Nothing moved. In the long grass the crickets sang. Down in the little woods an owl hooted. Across the meadow a dog barked. Miss Pinchon heard them all as she waited. The broom didn't budge. And then she heard the bells of St. Jude's toll the hour of midnight. Nothing happened. Neither deep breathing nor patient waiting seemed to animate the broom. "There must be more to it than this," Miss Pinchon muttered to herself. "But what?"

She unseated herself from the broom and dragged it off toward the house. As she moved away, a bat sailed off the top of the apple tree. "Well, at least there's *that!*" Miss Pinchon said. "It may be a good omen."

The following morning Miss Pinchon dressed in her best, a rusty dusty bombazine dress that she hadn't worn for many many years. It took some doing to get into it, because although Miss Pinchon wasn't a truly great cook, the foods she ate were starchy and more than adequate. Then she walked downtown to the library.

She caused no little stir. The librarians, usually quite contained and correct, whispered among themselves. The people in the reading room dropped their books and frankly stared. The fact was that Miss Pinchon had not visited the library in anyone's memory. Quite satisfied with the variety of stories in *Grimm's Fairy Tales* and *Pride and Prejudice*, she really had no need whatsoever to use the library. But today she was bent on a matter of research. She absolutely had to find out a few things about witches.

She selected several encyclopedias and an old book about witchcraft and took them over to a corner of the reading room, where she could be quite by herself. No one disturbed her and she read for several hours. If she had needed more evidence that she was indeed a witch, she certainly got it.

"Witches," the book said, "can be identified by several things. 1. They usually have a 'familiar,' a cat or bird, for instance, who is their constant companion."

"That's Gideon, of course," thought Miss Pinchon. And she read on.

"2. Witches indulge in the practice of walking backward against the sun, their hair flying loosely."

"Oh yes indeed!" thought Miss Pinchon, patting her straggling hair. "I walk backward in the garden all the time. Keeps the sun out of my eyes."

"3. Witches," the book continued, "have the peculiar inability to shed tears."

Miss Pinchon became thoughtful. "I can't remember when I've ever cried," she thought. "I may have when I was a baby, but no one ever said so."

Then Miss Pinchon went on to read about the history of witchcraft, the kinds of witches, spells, and charms. "Oh dear," she said to herself. "It's not all so very nice, is it?" But she took a little crumpled piece of paper from her bag and a stub of pencil, and licking the point thoughtfully, she looked carefully at the recipes for spells. "No, not that one! Oh dear, I wouldn't do *that*. It wouldn't be right or decent. Good heavens! Ah, here's one." And she made a few notes that she thought might be useful sometime.

And she saved for the last the thing that was

really first in her mind — transvection, which seemed to be the word the books used to describe the flight of witches. She was delighted to find some really helpful hints, such as it was best to leave the house through the chimney and — no wonder she had failed at first — to rub the body first with a very special ointment.

When Miss Pinchon had finished her work in the library she felt quite pleased. "Considering I'm trying to cram all this in very fast, I think I have got the hang of it," she said to herself as she walked home briskly. "The first thing to do, of course, is to get that broom working."

The Trouble with Brooms

V

Gideon was very irritable and restless when Miss Pinchon returned. He was not accustomed to being left alone for so long. "Dinner time," he said sulkily and then he shouted, "Give Gideon something to eat. To eat. To eat."

Miss Pinchon was apologetic. "I'm sorry, Gideon. But this matter took up my entire afternoon. There were some things I just had to find out. And really, it was well worth the trouble. You wait and see."

To make up for her neglect, she cooked pancakes and fed him bits with her fingers. She had always done this on special occasions, but it was interesting to discover in the witchcraft book that all witches hand-fed their "familiars." Gideon nipped her spitefully several times, but she didn't complain. She understood his mood quite well. When she had finished feeding Gideon she made herself some pancakes, burning them badly, but that was to be expected. She ate them anyway and enjoyed them enormously.

Then she began her preparations for the evening's flight. The recipe for the flying ointment was based on lard, and Miss Pinchon had some down in the cellar, where she kept things cold. There was one ingredient which she did not have — herb grace — but she had the oil of clove (she kept it for toothache), mace, and the pinch of salt. She mixed them all together into a sticky

mess and then, bringing it to a boil over the coal
stove, she said the magic words that would turn
it into a genuine flying ointment:

> *Salt and oil,*
> *Boil, boil.*
> *Clove and mace,*
> *Herb of grace.*
> *The devil's eye!*
> *The witch will fly!*

"I don't care for that bit about the devil's eye,"
muttered Miss Pinchon. "And what about that
herb grace? Well, never mind. Let's get on with
it." And she put the ointment to the side of the
stove to cool.

When it had cooled to a comfortable tepid
temperature, she dipped her fingers into it and
spread some on her arms. It was quite sticky and
not too pleasant a feeling, but it smelled deli-
cious. She smeared some on her face and then
took off her shoes and rubbed her feet. Then
she put on an old rain slicker and oiled that.

"Now for the hard part," she said, and stoop-
ing, she stepped into the fireplace and looked up.

It was an old house and had an enormous flue, which had once been able to accommodate the body of a chimney sweep . . . but they were usually small boys, and Miss Pinchon was a good-sized person.

"Oh, this is going to be very difficult," she said, "but climb I must." She took the broom and pushed it up the chimney ahead of her. A shower of soot fell on her head. It had been many a year since a chimney sweep had been in that chimney!

Miss Pinchon went back into the kitchen, got a small stool, and placed it in the fireplace. Then she climbed onto the stool and thrust the upper half of her body into the chimney. It was dark and airless, but along the side of the flue were steps of brick that enabled her to place her hands and feet in such a way that she could squeeze herself a bit farther into the chimney. After the first enormous effort Miss Pinchon was so tired — not to mention sticky and sooty — that she wasn't at all sure that she could go on. But she took a few deep breaths and climbed a bit more. The chimney seemed to get tighter and tighter.

"Oh dear," thought Miss Pinchon, "I may be stuck here." And then an advantage of the flying ointment became apparent. An unanointed Miss Pinchon might have stayed in the chimney forever, unseen and unmissed — except by Gideon, of course. But a well-greased Miss Pinchon managed to slip and slide her way up the chimney. She emerged, black and panting, and had to sit on the ridge of the roof to catch her breath.

Getting down from the roof was not as hard as one might think, because the main roof sloped down to the flat roof of the back porch, and it was possible for Miss Pinchon to slide down quite comfortably, pushing the broom ahead of her.

Once on the ground, Miss Pinchon wasted no time hurrying over to the shadow of the apple tree, where she quickly mounted the broom. The flying ointment on her hands made the broom a bit slippery, but she felt that that might be all to the good. The dark quiet of the garden and the brightness of the moon all went to make for a perfect flying climate. Miss Pinchon was ready. "I've got the flying ointment on," she said to herself. "I came out the chimney way. There

48

should be no further trouble with this now."

So she thought. But waiting quietly in the shadow of the apple tree and strongly willing herself to fly simply produced no results. Miss Pinchon did not become annoyed. But she was a bit puzzled.

"I might need a bit of a head start," she thought, so she started an even-paced trot around the garden, every once in a while making a small leap into the air, but earthbound she remained.

Once more she ran and once more she leaped, and finally she came to a dead stop in front of the Lady Perchpetal chrysanthemums, thoroughly and utterly perplexed. Then, from behind the chrysanthemums, something moved.

Miss Pinchon turned her head quickly, became wary, and stared at the chrysanthemums. Had she imagined it? It might have been a bat. She had almost come to that conclusion when it moved again. Miss Pinchon got off the broom and used it to poke aside the chrysanthemum heads. They parted to reveal a quaking Zigmund Hutchmaier.

At first Miss Pinchon was speechless. Then she started to waggle her head and mutter and stamp her feet, and it is probable that she would have whacked Zigmund with the broom were it not that she would have destroyed the enormous and magnificent chrysanthemums. Finally, when Miss Pinchon had sputtered herself out, she said in a voice vibrating with feeling, "Come out!"

Zigmund crawled out onto the grass in front of the chrysanthemums and regarded with awe, and at close range, the neighborhood witch. In

the dark, wielding a broom, with the moon behind her, her face mobile with rage and shining
with flying ointment, she was the most witchly
witch he had ever imagined. Tears welled in his
eyes.

"What are you doing?" demanded Miss
Pinchon, her voice going from high to low and
back again from lack of use. She cleared her
throat.

"Only looking," said Zigmund faintly.

"Only *stealing* is more like it. Only stealing
my chrysanthemums, you dreadful boy," and she
waved the broom again and Zigmund put his
hands up over his head.

"No ma'am, I wasn't stealing. Honest. I was
watching you fly around on your broom, that's
all."

Miss Pinchon stopped short. "Flying?" she
asked. "You saw me flying?"

"Yes ma'am. I couldn't help it. I just happened to be standing here and then I saw you
flying."

Miss Pinchon dismissed as unimportant how
and why Zigmund just happened to be standing there when everyone else was in bed. She

pressed her question. "You actually *saw* me fly?"

Zigmund nodded, and then he said, "Well, I guess I saw you come down anyway. Maybe I didn't really see you in the air."

Miss Pinchon pouted. "That's because I *wasn't* in the air," she said, and stamped her foot again. Then she wheeled on Zigmund. "If you thought you saw me flying, why aren't you surprised? Didn't it amaze you to see someone flying?"

"No, ma'am. It didn't amaze me to see *you* flying. I always knew witches could fly," and then he clapped his hand over his mouth as he realized the tactlessness of his remark. He waited for Miss Pinchon to go into another rage, but she was too interested in Zigmund's observations.

"But it *looked* to you as though I was flying?"

"It looked that way. Yes, ma'am."

Then Miss Pinchon stamped and threw the broom down. "Well, I wasn't!" And then she said almost pleadingly, "I can't get the infernal thing off the ground." After that she got so depressed that she just stared off into the darkness of the hedge, with a very great sadness in her face.

Zigmund took advantage of the quiet moment to retreat to a safer distance, but he was too fascinated to take the opportunity to flee.

"What's the matter?" he inquired, getting back some of his usual boldness. "Broom break down?"

Miss Pinchon came out of her reverie and stooped to pick up the broom. She shook it impatiently. "Oh," she said, "I don't know what's the matter. It just won't fly."

Zigmund came a little closer and peered at the broom. "I can't see how it ever did," he said frankly. "It doesn't seem to have anything to *make* it fly." He stared at it a while. "Maybe it's like an old car. You have to give it a kind of push or something."

Miss Pinchon was interested. "How a push?" she asked.

Zigmund's agile mind was churning now. "Like if you get on it and I sort of push you," he said.

Miss Pinchon was eager. "Maybe you're right," she said. "Insufficient kinetic power, perhaps. All right. Do you want to try now?"

So Miss Pinchon mounted the broom once more and Zigmund said, "Okay now, start running and I'll be pushing."

Miss Pinchon started a slow loping run around the garden, building up steam until she was pelting up and down the garden paths amid the asters and the marigolds, with Zigmund pushing with all his might in the rear.

"I didn't know witches were so slippery," Zigmund puffed, as his hands slid about on Miss Pinchon's slicker.

"It's the flying ointment," yelled Miss Pinchon.

"Maybe you need more of it then," suggested Zigmund.

But after seven exhausting minutes Miss Pinchon panted, "It's no use. I can't run any-more," and slowed to a walk. Zigmund chugged to a halt and they both sank to the grass, gasping for breath.

"Just for a minute there," puffed Zigmund, "I thought I had her going."

"Did you really?" gasped Miss Pinchon hope-fully.

"I really did," Zigmund said. "It needs just a little something else. Hey!" he suddenly ex-claimed. "I have an idea. Listen," he said to Miss Pinchon. "Would it be all right if I asked a friend of mine to help? He has something I think we could use."

"Now?" asked Miss Pinchon.

"No," said Zigmund, "he'd be asleep now. I'll see if I can get him over tomorrow after school."

"No," Miss Pinchon said sharply. "I don't want to do this in the daytime — at least not until I'm experienced anyway. It will have to be by moonlight."

"All right," said Zigmund. "I'll try and get here tomorrow night with my friend. I guess I'd better be going now before my mother starts creeping around the house tucking in everyone's covers. Good night."

"Good night," said Miss Pinchon, and got up and went toward the house. Gideon was asleep and she blessed her luck for that. She didn't feel like any more talk tonight.

Bells and Spells | VI

Miss Pinchon had plenty of second thoughts in the morning and all through the next day. She wasn't at all sure she wanted Zigmund's help, let alone that of his friend. Who were they anyhow? How did she know she could trust them? She was used to spending most of her time in her own company or Gideon's, and did not really like the idea of expanding her circle of acquaintances quite that much or that fast. But then she won-

dered if she would be able to manage *without*
their help. Well, she didn't know. And then on
the other hand . . . and so on. By nightfall she had
decided to tell Zigmund to forget the whole affair
and, furthermore, to stay out of the chrysanthemums in the future.

She thought about that while she smeared on
the flying ointment, and fretted about it as she
squeezed herself up through the chimney. The
slide down the roof, however, turned out to be
quite a delight now that the uncertainty was out
of it, and when she finally climbed down from
the back porch into the garden Miss Pinchon was
in the throes of mixed emotions — irate at the
thought of Zigmund in the chrysanthemums,
confused about accepting his offer of help, and
altogether jubilant from the exhilarating slide
down the roof.

Miss Pinchon mumbled to herself as she
crossed the garden, broom in hand. "I'll just tell
him to be off, that's all. Both him *and* his friend.
That's what I'll do." And then she lifted her
head to see Zigmund, himself, standing beneath
the apple tree, and beside him the largest kite
she had ever seen.

"My word!" exclaimed Miss Pinchon, forgetting her resolve to rid herself of Zigmund. "What's that for? And where's your friend?"

"Here he is," said Zigmund, and he pulled a tall boy from behind the kite. "This is Jacques Geordi. He's sort of new in the neighborhood. This is his kite."

"Hello," said Jacques, but he seemed a bit nervous and stepped halfway behind the kite.

Miss Pinchon peered closely at him. "How do," she muttered.

Then Jacques said, "This is my little sister, Lucy," and he pushed a small girl halfway out from behind the other side of the kite.

Miss Pinchon stared at Lucy, and Lucy retreated behind the kite again. "You didn't say you were bringing *two* friends," Miss Pinchon protested to Zigmund.

"I couldn't bring Jacques without Lucy," said Zigmund hurriedly. "He's supposed to look after her tonight. Their mother had to go away to see her aunt and. . . ."

"Oh, all right," said Miss Pinchon reluctantly, "but remember, this isn't a public affair." She shook her finger at them sternly. "Not a word of

this outside this garden! Do you understand?"

"Yes, ma'am," said Zigmund.

"Yes, ma'am," said Jacques.

"Yes, ma'am," Lucy whispered from behind the kite.

"All right, then," said Miss Pinchon. "What's your idea?"

"Well, here's the thing," said Zigmund, stepping forward and taking command. "My idea is that you are fighting too much gravity. We have got to combat that by starting your flight from a higher point. See?"

"Yes," said Miss Pinchon hopefully. "That does make sense. What point are you thinking of? I just came down from the roof."

"That would have been a pretty good place," said Jacques, gathering a little courage and leaving the protection of the kite. "But it might be hard to get back up. We thought of the apple tree. It's easy to climb."

"I've done it often," boasted Zigmund.

"You have!" said Miss Pinchon. "When?" And as Zigmund looked confused, she answered the question herself. "When it was full of apples this summer, I'm sure. Well never mind that now. When I'm up that apple tree, what then?"

"Besides using the tree to get you off the ground to oppose the pull of gravity," Zigmund said, "we're going to provide an upward pull by attaching Jacques' kite to you. This will give you a good enough start so that you can go on all by yourself."

"Hm," said Miss Pinchon, impressed with Zigmund's confidence. "It does seem to make sense. Rather like priming a pump. Well, all right. I'll do it, but. . . ."

"What's the trouble?" asked Zigmund. "You have nothing to worry about. We're doing all the work. All you have to do is get up the tree and follow directions."

"Well, I was just thinking," said Miss Pinchon, "I don't suppose there is any problem getting down again?"

"Of course not," said Zigmund. "Down is the easy part."

It was with difficulty that Miss Pinchon climbed to the upper branches of the apple tree. It is all very well for young boys to climb trees, but a middle-aged lady, of stout build, in a rain slicker

covered with flying ointment, doesn't find it all
that easy. But Jacques, Zigmund, and Lucy
pushed with a will and before too long, bearing
only a few scratches, Miss Pinchon was settled
side-saddle on a limb halfway up the tree, broom
ready, poised for flight. The moon shining
through the branches caught the silvery lights of
her hair, reflected in her shining slicker, and
touched the yellow straws of the broom.

She waited in the tree while the children concentrated on launching the kite. A good gust of wind enabled them to get it off to a fine start, and they reeled and unreeled the line with marvelous skill until the enormous kite was sailing high and unseen in the darkness. It took considerable tugging from both Jacques and Zigmund to hold it, so it was Lucy who made her way up the tree to tie the kite string to Miss Pinchon's belt. Then Lucy climbed down again.

"Now," called Zigmund from the ground, "whenever you're ready, jump as high as you can, and you're off!"

"Oh, marvelous!" cried Miss Pinchon. "I'll be all set in a moment." And she adjusted her skirt, wedged the broomstick firmly between her knees, and took a deep breath.

Now in the next instant three things happened in very quick order. Miss Pinchon leaped into the air and started treading the air with her legs, exactly like a swimmer treading water. At just that moment the bells of St. Jude's began to chime the hour of midnight. And within a breath of time after that, Miss Pinchon came crashing down, broomstick and all, into a con-

venient pile of salt hay piled up for mulching the garden.

When Jacques, Zigmund, and Lucy rushed to where she lay, no sound or movement came from the pile of salt hay.

"Is she dead?" Lucy whispered in fright.

"No," growled Miss Pinchon, "I'm not dead." She sat up, and then she started to mutter and sputter as of old. "The bells!" she muttered, and then she raised her voice and said again, "The bells! The confounded church bells!"

"Should you say that about church bells?" asked Jacques worriedly.

"I can say anything I like. I'm a witch, don't forget."

"What about the bells?" asked Zigmund, helping her to her feet.

"Oh, it's my own fault. I should have thought of it. But it's just like everything else I do . . . backfires. Bells!" she exclaimed again. "Church bells are one of the few things that can make witches fall right out of the sky when they're flying. Never fails. That's why, when there were so many witches around, they used to ring the church bells all night. Kept the witches away. I should have realized it was nearly midnight and the bells would ring any minute. Oh dear, this is going to be another one of those things that just fizzles. Well, I'm too sore to try that again for a while," and she rubbed her bruises as she spoke. "Anyway, I didn't really feel much strength in that kite. I rather had the feeling I was pulling it down rather than it pulling me up."

"Impossible," said Jacques. "Not that kite. Why I can scarcely pull it in. Look." He released the string from Miss Pinchon's belt, and Zigmund and he pulled and reeled, while Miss Pinchon continued to nurse her aches and bruises and Lucy stood by shaking her head sympathetically.

"Well, I was right about one thing," Zigmund said. "Coming down *was* the easy part."

When the kite was finally pulled down and Miss Pinchon had had time to think and compose herself, she said, "You know, it's just barely possible that I may not be a flying type of witch, after all — a *striga*, I think they called them in the encyclopedia. I may be something more like a sorceress — something with charms and spells and all that. Maybe I should try turning someone into something or other." She looked at Lucy. "Is there anything you would rather be than a girl?" she asked. "A rabbit or anything?"

Lucy looked nervous. "Rabbits are very nice," she said, "but right now I'd rather be a girl, if you please." And then she added, "I have a brand-new dress anyway."

"How about either of you?" Miss Pinchon asked Zigmund and Jacques. "I could try turning you into horses. Boys like horses."

"I like horses all right," said Jacques, "but I don't want to be one."

"Me neither," said Zigmund.

Miss Pinchon pouted. "I'm just being courteous asking you," she said. "I don't have to have your permission, you know."

"We know," said Zigmund.

"Oh, I have it!" Miss Pinchon cried suddenly. "I'll transform Estella, that nasty cow of Mr.

Bodenheimer's. I'll change her into a dog. That will serve them both right. Eating my chrysanthemums!"

"*Now* you're talking!" cried Zigmund. "Go ahead."

"Oh no!" said Lucy. "I'm scared."

"Don't listen to her," said Jacques. "It's okay. Go ahead."

"Well, let me see if I can remember the spell," Miss Pinchon said, thinking back to the notes she had taken in the library. She thought quietly for a few minutes, and then suddenly she took a deep breath and held it until her eyes started to bulge. Then she slowly let her breath out, and while she was exhaling she waved her arms in the air and hissed:

> *Bulldog grinning,*
> *Whirlwind spinning,*
> *Church bells dinning,*
> *Sinners sinning,*
> *Devil winning,*
> *Change beginning!*

"Well that's done it!" Miss Pinchon said gleefully. "Shall we go and see?"

Together the four walked through the little
wood that divided Miss Pinchon's garden from
Mr. Boo's field, and together they crept quietly
through the field of dried grass to the barn
where Estella lived.

"You look," Miss Pinchon said, pushing Zigmund ahead of her. "I'm too excited. This is
my first transformation, you know."

Zigmund opened the barn door a crack and it creaked dangerously. They waited nervously to see if they had awakened Mr. Boo, but nothing happened. Zigmund pushed the door a bit more and the moonlight flooded the stall to reveal the sulky Estella, now asleep on her feet, as cows are accustomed to doze, unchanged even to her markings.

"Oh dear," mourned Miss Pinchon. "What did I do wrong? Let's see, I may have left something out. Bulldog, whirlwind, church bells, sinners. No, that's everything. Dear, dear! Can't I even do a simple transformation?"

She was terribly depressed all the way back to the house, where she bid the children good night.

"Don't feel bad," said Lucy. "Maybe you'll do something tomorrow."

"Of course," said Miss Pinchon, but she felt quite weary.

"Honestly," said Zigmund, when she had gone into the house. "I'm sort of sorry for her. She's a witch with no know-how."

Raising a Storm | VII

Gideon was furious the next morning. He seemed to know more about what was going on than one would think.

"I do believe you're jealous," said Miss Pinchon, somewhat flattered.

"Witch! Witch!" yelled Gideon.

"Never mind that," said Miss Pinchon, detecting some sarcasm in Gideon's tone. "Just because I didn't fly doesn't mean a thing. Just because I didn't succeed in the transformation doesn't mean anything either. There's more than one kind of witch in the world, as you very well know. It's only a question of discovering just what kind of witch I am. Besides, you're a 'familiar,' and do you do any noticeable magic? No! Are you running any diabolical errands? No!

"Well," she said, softening her tone as she saw that Gideon was genuinely hurt, "it's not your fault any more than it is mine. We have both come to it late in life."

She cheerfully broke three dishes at breakfast, and then on an impulse rolled out some cookies just in case the children came over to help again. The cookies burned, of course, but they looked fairly good anyway. Miss Pinchon fed Gideon a few, which he accepted grudgingly.

By the time she had finished there was not much time for the garden, but she pulled some weeds around the chrysanthemums, though her heart wasn't in it. She was thinking about what she should try next. The ground in the garden was very dry from the summer drought, and the fall rains had not come as they should. And then, all of a sudden, Miss Pinchon knew what she must do.

"I'll cause a storm!" she cried. "Of course! That's just what's needed, and it certainly can't be nearly as difficult as flying or changing cows into dogs." And she stopped the weeding and hurried back to the house to go over her library notes.

"I've got to get it just right," she said as she hunted for the bits of paper. "I know I copied down some ways to make a storm. Ah, here it is. Well, good! I'll have those flowers watered before evening. My, I'm glad I thought of that. And none of that sticky flying ointment needed for this!"

Miss Pinchon was just about to go outside when Gideon started to squawk in a sulky tone.

"Now what?" she asked, and went in and got Gideon some grapes, which he liked a great deal. As she fed him she thought, "Perhaps he would be happier if he were in on what we are doing." So she unfastened the chain on his perch and allowed him to jump onto her shoulder, and they went out into the garden together. Gideon seemed much pleased with the whole thing, and showed it by not saying a single unpleasant word.

As soon as Miss Pinchon and Gideon appeared at the door, Zigmund pushed his head through the hedge. It seemed as if he had just been sitting there waiting, but Miss Pinchon did not flatter herself that much. She chalked it up to coincidence.

"Hey!" called Zigmund.

"How do," said Miss Pinchon. "You're just in time. I'm going to conjure up a storm."

"No kidding!" cried Zigmund. "I'll go get Jacques and Lucy." And he did.

Everyone was introduced to Gideon, who looked at them all suspiciously and then turned his back on them. But he held his tongue.

"He's really not used to company," said Miss Pinchon, excusing his bad manners, at which Gideon flew off her shoulder and perched in the apple tree.

"Are you really going to make a storm?" asked Lucy.

"Yes, indeed," said Miss Pinchon. "A good big storm, too. We need it. It's a wonder I didn't

think of it before. Everything is bone dry and in
need of a good wet."

"How are you going to do it?" asked Jacques.

"Well, there are several methods," said Miss
Pinchon, "but I thought I'd just get me a willow
wand and beat the stream a bit. Simplest way.
Nothing to it. We'll have a storm in no time.
Really I must be simple-minded not to have
tried this first. But then, I was so caught up in
that flying idea. Well. . . ." and she led the way

to a small stream that ran through the little wood at the edge of her garden.

"I just hope that stream hasn't dried up entirely," muttered Miss Pinchon, taking such big strong strides that the children had to run to keep up with her. Gideon flew along over her head, enjoying himself enormously.

At the edge of the stream a willow tree grew, and danced the ballet that only willow trees know. Miss Pinchon reached up to one of the low branches and broke off a long wand. She flexed it and whipped it through the air, and it made a marvelous whistling sound. "That's just the thing," she said.

"Now we'll all go down to the edge of the stream, and I'll just perform this simple ceremony, and that's all there is to it." And she slid down the small bank followed closely by the children.

"Maybe I should go back and get my raincoat," said Lucy. "Mama won't want me to get all wet."

"Never mind," said Jacques. "You didn't know it was going to rain. She can't blame you for that."

"But I know it now," said Lucy.

"No time for that," Miss Pinchon said. "Here we go."

Miss Pinchon lifted the willow wand high in the air and brought it down with a resounding whack upon the peacefully moving surface of the shallow stream. Water splashed on all of them. Then she raised the wand again and brought it down once more, and then again and again. And while she did it, she chanted in a low voice:

Hum mum numb scum
Biddle diddle rains come.
Winds rise,
Clouds break,
Lizard, turtle,
Toad and snake,
Owl and raven,
Bat and mouse,
Storm descend on
Field and house.
Hum mum numb scum
Biddle diddle rains come.

When she had finished the chant Miss Pinchon turned around to the children and gave them a pleasant smile that smacked a bit of self-satisfaction. "I didn't leave out a thing," she said. "Let's hurry back before we get soaked." She gathered the children together, beckoned to Gideon, and they raced through the garden and up to the back porch.

"Wait here," said Miss Pinchon. "I'll get some cookies and we can sit out here on the porch and eat them while we watch the storm."

The children caught their breath while Miss Pinchon was in the house, and Gideon settled himself on the porch rail and preened his feathers. "Toad and snake," he muttered. "Bat and mouse." And Lucy was glad Miss Pinchon didn't hear him because he sounded a bit taunting, she thought.

Miss Pinchon came out with the burned cookies, and they ate them hungrily. Lucy thought the burn had a special witch-like taste and was quite good. Zigmund and Jacques ate twenty-three between them. Gideon had two. Miss Pinchon didn't notice how many she ate. She was watching the sky.

The afternoon sun was low and bright. The air was dry. A loud bee made the silent air hum. The leaves waited, but no rain came. Miss Pinchon and the children went down into the garden and scanned the sky. There wasn't a useful cloud to be seen. They waited another hour, and when dusk fell it began to occur to them all that the spell was not going to work.

The Magic Touch | VIII

Miss Pinchon was very depressed. She sat cross-legged on the grass in front of the Lady Perch-petal chrysanthemums, and would have wept were it not impossible because of her being a witch.

"I don't seem to be much of a sorceress," she said miserably. Lucy nodded her head in agreement. "Obviously I'm not a very successful flying type of witch," Miss Pinchon continued.

"Obviously," agreed Zigmund and Jacques.

"I never even entertained the idea of being a mean *maleficia* — all that evil eye business and rending of black lambs and poisoning and so forth. That's just too nasty. So *what* kind of witch can I be?" And then a terrible thought occurred to her, and her eyes opened wide with horror as she contemplated it. "Suppose," she said, looking from one to the other wildly, "just suppose I'm not really a witch at all!"

There was an instant's pause, and then they all burst out laughing at the obvious nonsense of Miss Pinchon's remark. They laughed and laughed, and when Zigmund got his breath he said, "Don't worry about *that*," and started laughing again. Miss Pinchon, despite her depression, was forced to admit it was ridiculous and joined in the laughter. Gideon, from his perch on the kitchen porch, laughed hoarsely and mirthlessly.

"All right," said Miss Pinchon, finally recovering her composure and getting to her feet. "Be that as it may, I have got to clip those large chrysanthemum heads before they pull over the whole plant. I have to get some more weeding done. I have got to divide those perennials before the frost. I've been much too neglectful of the garden all these days, concentrating on all that witch stuff and forgetting all about my main work.

"After all," she went on, talking to herself as of old, "the garden is the only thing I do that doesn't fall to pieces in my hands, that doesn't jump about if I touch it. After all, who still has flowers in their garden now except me? Sometimes, when I look at this garden," she said, turning to Lucy and speaking rather confidentially and a bit shyly, "I have to confess I think I do have a completely superior and unusually marvelous way with flowers. A green thumb. A magic touch, as they say."

"*What* did you say!" exclaimed Lucy, just as Zigmund and Jacques said, "Say that again!"

"A magic touch," said Miss Pinchon obligingly, and then she stopped cutting Lady Perchpetals and stood with her mouth open, looking from one to the other.

"A magic touch!" she said again, and then she whispered, "Is *that* it?" Then her wrinkled face broke into smiles. "That's it! That's it! I feel it. I'm a flower witch. I'm a flower witch!"

"Witch of the flowers," said Lucy. "How lovely!"

"Oh how marvelous!" exclaimed Miss Pinchon. "It's like being born all over again. I'm a flower witch!" And she hopped about joyously, and suddenly leaped up and down and into the air with amazing agility for one of her age and build.

"Hey!" cried Jacques. "Were you flying just then? I was sure you were flying."

"I don't think so," said Miss Pinchon, leaping again. "It's more jumping than flying, but it's quite fun."

Then everybody tried leaping and jumping a bit, and Jacques kept insisting that Miss Pinchon went up much farther than any of them, which, he said, was a sign that perhaps she might still, with practice, make it as a flying witch.

"Perhaps," said Miss Pinchon, "but if so, it will just be an added feature. There are plenty of flying witches — the books are full of them — but I am the only flower witch that I have ever heard of."

"Witch! Witch! Witch!" yelled Gideon from the porch.

"Oh, I would love to be a flower witch," said Lucy. "More than anything."

"Would you?" asked Miss Pinchon, quite pleased. "I'll take you on as an apprentice then. I'll show you everything."

"Oh, thank you!" exclaimed Lucy.

"How about us?" asked Zigmund.

"Very well, the three of you. But you'll have to work and there's a great deal to learn."

Just then there was a clap of thunder and a flash of lightning, and then the rain came down in a torrent.

"Well," cried Miss Pinchon, as they ran to the shelter of the porch, "at *last* that spell is working! It certainly took its time."

"Toad and snake," Gideon said. "Bat and mouse." But this time he sounded almost respectful.

About the Author

Felice Holman was born in New York City. She attended Drew Seminary in Carmel, New York, and received her B.A. degree from Syracuse University. She first appeared in print as a poet, and her work was published in anthologies while she was still a student at Syracuse University. She has worked as a free-lance writer and as a fashion copywriter. Miss Holman is the author of the popular "Elisabeth" books. Some of her most recent books are: *Victoria's Castle*; *Professor Diggins' Dragons*; and *Silently, the Cat, and Miss Theodosia*, which was cited by the *New York Times* as one of the outstanding children's books of the year. Miss Holman lives in Westport, Connecticut, with her husband and daughter.

About the Artist

Arnold Lobel was born in Los Angeles and grew up in Schenectady, New York. He is a graduate of Pratt Institute. Mr. Lobel is the illustrator of *Dudley Pippin* and the author/illustrator of *Martha, the Movie Mouse*; *A Zoo for Mister Muster*; and *Giant John*. He lives in Brooklyn with his wife and two children.

FIC
H

Holman, Felice
The witch on the corner

Date Due

SEP 2 4 2014 Meghan 6th			

1091

For a time, Miss Pinchon bewitches the
entire neighborhood. But when she realizes
she possesses powers of witchcraft, things
are never the same in her life.